First Grade Elves

by Joanne Ryder
Pictures by Betsy Lewin

Troll Associates

Library of Congress Cataloging-in-Publication Data

Ryder, Joanne.
    First grade elves / by Joanne Ryder; pictures by Betsy Lewin.
        p.   cm.—(First grade is the best!)
    Summary: To celebrate Christmas, Hanukkah, and Kwanzaa, the
students in Mrs. Lee's first grade class act as secret elves, doing
good deeds for one another.
    ISBN 0-8167-3010-5 (lib. bdg.)   ISBN 0-8167-3011-3 (pbk.)
    [1. Conduct of life—Fiction.   2. Christmas—Fiction.
3. Hanukkah—Fiction.   4. Kwanzaa—Fiction.   5. Schools—Fiction.]
I. Lewin, Betsy, ill.   II. Title.   III. Series.
PZ7.R959Fk   1994
[E]—dc20   93-25543

Text copyright © 1994 Joanne Ryder

Illustration copyright © 1994 Betsy Lewin

One December day, there were new
decorations in the first grade classroom.

"Look," said Gabe, "our own
Christmas tree."

"And candles for Hanukkah," said
Robin. "It's our festival of lights."

"We have candles for Kwanzaa," said Lisa. "We remember our African heritage by lighting candles and telling traditional stories."

"Everyone has lovely ways to celebrate this special time," said Mrs. Lee. "It's nice to share them all."

"In my family we have secret elves," said Matt. "We pick a name and do nice things for that person. My elf made my bed this morning."

"I'd like to be a secret elf," said Meg.

"I know a way you can all be secret elves and do kind things for each other," said Mrs. Lee.

"Let's make some special snowflakes," Mrs. Lee said. "The snowflakes can be our secret sign. Whenever you do something nice, leave one behind. We'll know a secret elf was here."

The next day, Robin found her lost mitten and a snowflake.

"Thank you, secret elf," she said.

"Look," cried Meg. "An elf left me some stickers."

"Me, too," said Lisa. "Thanks, elf."

Mrs. Lee saw a painting on her
desk. When she picked it up, there
was a snowflake underneath.

She smiled at all the elves in her
class.

Matt couldn't find his homework.
"I think I left it at home," he said.
But it was on his table after recess.
"An elf must have found it," said
Lisa, "but there's no snowflake."

The next few days, the first grade classroom was full of elves.

An elf put a handmade dinosaur in Brian's pocket.

An elf left Gabe a shark pen rolled inside a snowflake.

Inside Matt's cubby, there wasn't any snowflake, but there was a shiny red plane.

Sometimes everyone got a surprise.
''Chocolate coins!'' cried Katie.
''That's a Hanukkah treat,'' said
Mrs. Lee, ''from one of our elves.''

"Can we leave some treats for the animals?" asked Katie.

"My grandma makes a holiday tree for the birds," said Gabe. "It's full of the food they like to eat."

Mrs. Lee and the children decorated a tree outside.

They hung doughnuts, chunks of oranges, and chains of popcorn on the branches. They sprinkled sunflower seeds on the ground.

The children watched birds and squirrels visit their tree.

"I wonder if they know who gave them the food," said Nick.

"Maybe the animals think little
elves did," said Brian.

"They did," said Meg. "First grade
elves!"

At recess, Matt waved to his twin.
Mike was in another first grade class.

"Look what my elf left me," said
Matt. "At least I think it was my elf.
I didn't get a snowflake, but I got lots
of peanuts. Want some?"

"Thanks," said Mike, grinning.
"You sure have a great elf."

Just before vacation, the children had a special day. The first graders wore elf hats. They sang songs and made gifts to take home.

After lunch there was a plate of
cookies and a card from Mrs. Lee.

"For the sweetest first grade elves,"
Lisa read. "Thanks for your kind
deeds."

"I liked being an elf," said Meg, eating a star cookie.

"It was fun to be surprised," said Gabe.

"Can I ask who found my mitten now?" said Robin.

"I did," said Brian. "Martha was sleeping on it."

"Who gave us the stickers?" said
Meg and Lisa.

"I did," said Mrs. Lee.

They gave her a two-elf hug.

Brian found out Katie made the green dinosaur for him. Nick had given Gabe the shark pen.

"But who found my homework?" Matt asked. "Who gave me the neat plane and the peanuts?"

Nobody answered. Nobody knew.

"Matt, here's an envelope with your name on it," said Nick.

"Open this and find your secret elf," Matt read.

Inside was a piece of shiny paper. Matt looked at it and smiled at what he saw.

"I know who my elf is now," he told Mrs. Lee. "Can I get him?"

Mrs. Lee nodded. Matt ran out of the room.

"It's Mike!" cried Katie.

"You were right," Matt told his twin. "I do have a great secret elf."

"Happy holidays," said Mrs. Lee, "to all our first grade elves."

Let it Snow!

You can turn scrap paper into wonderful snowflakes. For your first snowflake, use a large sheet of paper. It's easier to cut. It's fun to make smaller ones later on. You will need some child-safe scissors, too.

If your paper is not square, fold it like this and cut off the extra piece.

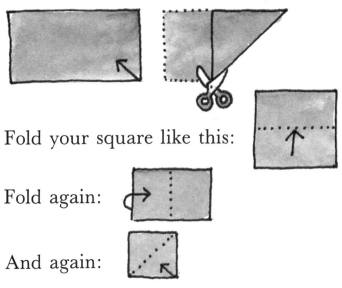

Fold your square like this:

Fold again:

And again:

Until it looks like this:

Cut along the dotted lines.

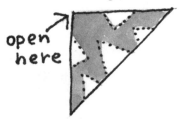

open here

Unfold the paper.
Watch your
snowflake appear!

Now make another snowflake with
your own design. You might cut half
circles, skinny slits, or fat triangles
along the edges of your folded paper.
Leave some space between each
cut-out shape.

Make snowflakes to hang in your
room, to decorate cards and gifts, or
to leave for your friends as the first
grade elves did.